Because of Music!

WRITTEN BY

MOSES A. HARDIE, III

ILLUSTRATED BY

CHRIS HOUSE

Dedications

This story is dedicated to the toe-tappers and finger-snappers, the head-bobbers and the pop-lockers, the beat-makers and the body-shakers... dedicated to the rhythm, the pulse, the music...

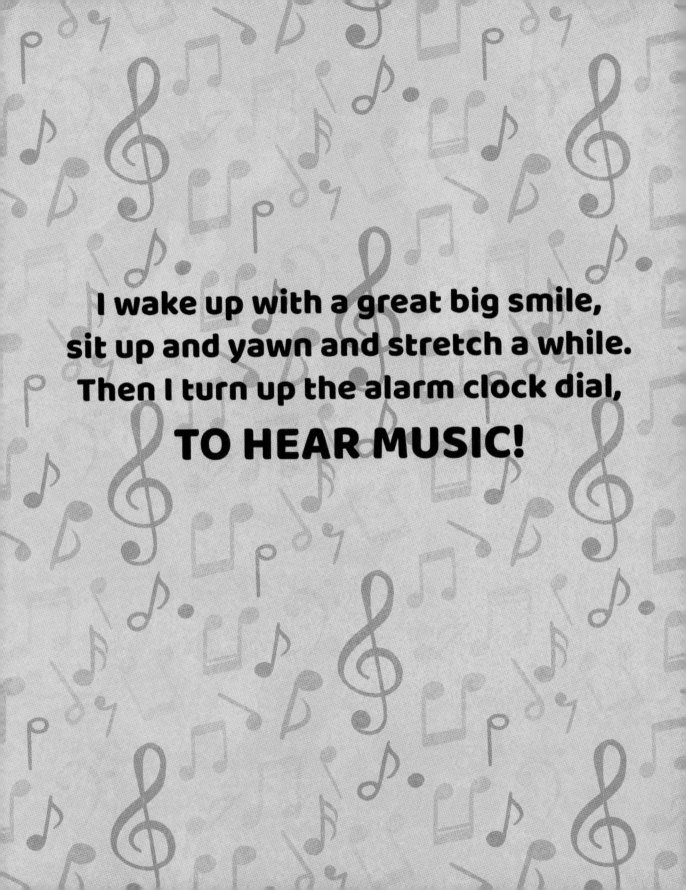

I wake up with a great big smile,
sit up and yawn and stretch a while.
Then I turn up the alarm clock dial,

TO HEAR MUSIC!

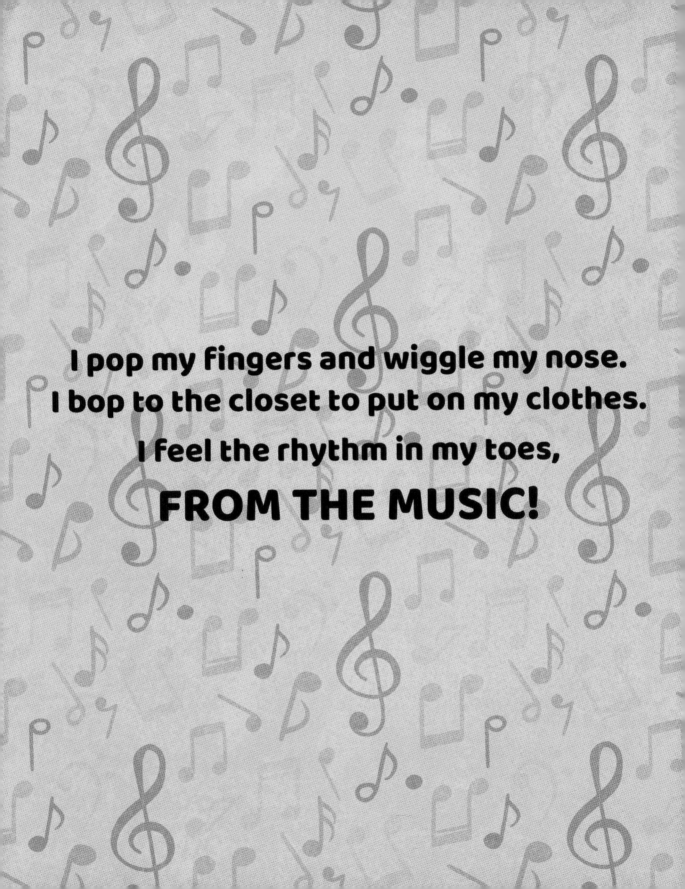

I pop my fingers and wiggle my nose.
I bop to the closet to put on my clothes.
I feel the rhythm in my toes,

FROM THE MUSIC!

I'm feelin' good, I'm feelin' fine,
I hear mama say it's breakfast time.
When that song ends
I'll press rewind,

TO HEAR MORE MUSIC!

The bacon pops and the sizzle of the eggs both match the rhythm that's in my legs,
I just can't help but nod my head.

I GOT THE MUSIC!

Outside I hear the cars go pass,
some drivin' slow, some drivin' fast.
When they roll down their
window glass,

I HEAR MUSIC!

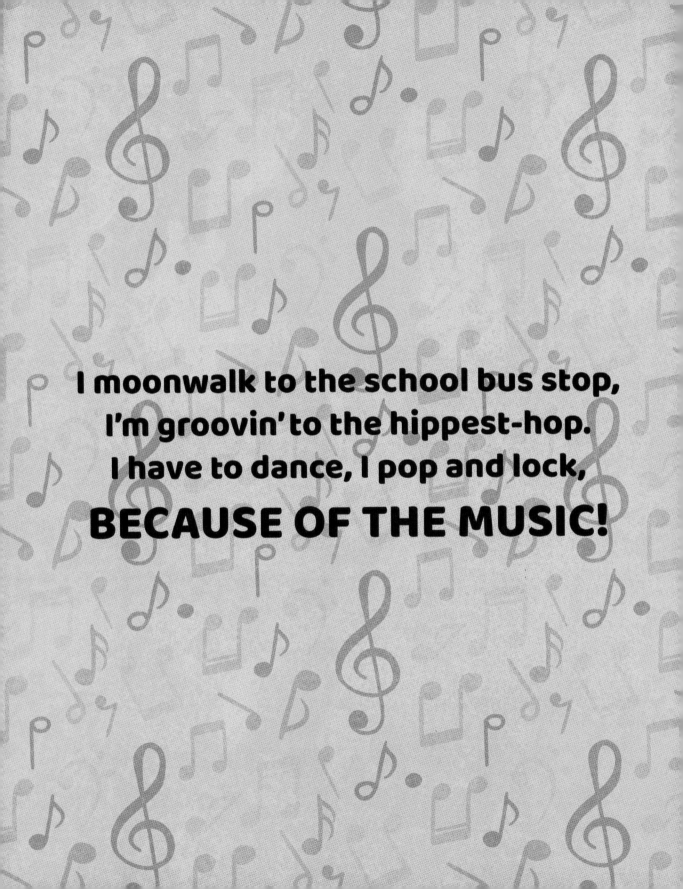

I moonwalk to the school bus stop,
I'm groovin' to the hippest-hop.
I have to dance, I pop and lock,
BECAUSE OF THE MUSIC!

When I get on the bus to school,
I keep on dancin', my moves are cool.
I'm movin' like a dancin' fool.
IT'S ALL ABOUT THE MUSIC!

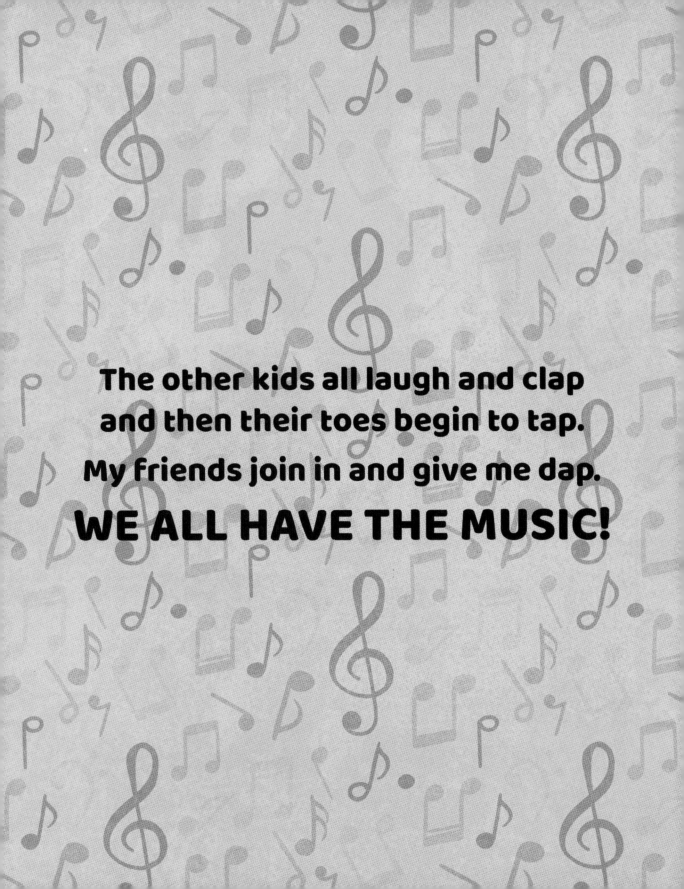

The other kids all laugh and clap
and then their toes begin to tap.

My friends join in and give me dap.

WE ALL HAVE THE MUSIC!

In class I try to hold it inside,
but the rhythm is really hard to hide.
I just can't wait to get outside,

TO GROOVE TO THE MUSIC!

At dinner Daddy's fork and spoon, they hit the plate and make a tune. I'll be jammin' to bed soon,

TO DREAM ABOUT THE MUSIC!

At bedtime Mommy sees me swayin',
and says "but there's no music playin'."
It's in my soul and that's
where it's stayin'.
I LOVE THE MUSIC!